USBORNE

Quest of the Gods

With thanks to Adrian Bott

First published in the UK in 2012 by Usborne Publishing Ltd.,
Usborne House, 83-85 Saffron Hill, London EC1N 8RT, England.
www.usborne.com

Text copyright © Hothouse Fiction, 2012

Illustrations copyright © Usborne Publishing Ltd., 2012

Illustrations by Jerry Parris

Map by Ian McNee

The name Usborne and the devices ♀ ⊕ are Trade Marks of
Usborne Publishing Ltd.

A CIP catalogue record for this book is available from the British Library.

ISBN 9781409521075   JFMAM JASOND/12   02357/1

Printed in Dongguan, Guangdong, China.

BATTLE OF THE
CROCODILE KING

DAN HUNTER

USBORNE

THE PROPHECY OF THE SPHINX

The Sphinx am I
Guardian of the Pyramids
Keeper of Secrets

The past I remember
The present I see
The future I foretell

When the Pharaoh shall die
At the hands of his son
A plague shall fall upon Egypt

The Lord of Storms will rise again
The good Gods will be chained
And monsters will walk the land

The Sacred River shall slow and dry
The sun will scorch the land like fire
The streets of Egypt shall run with blood

But hope will come from the south
A hero of the wheatfields
A king without a kingdom

The last of his family
A lost child of Horus
He shall battle the monsters to free the Gods

He will claim the White Crown
He will claim the Red Crown
He will rule all Egypt

The Sphinx am I
These secrets I share
Guard them well

MANU'S MAP OF ANCIENT EGYPT

NILE DELTA

Heliopolis

Giza

Saqqara

RED SEA

Temple of Set

EASTERN DESERT

Nubt

HIGH DESERT

Waset and Karnak

Entrance to the
Underworld

Temple of Horus

Nebyt

Fortress of Fire

THE NILE

N

S

SAHARA DESERT

PROLOGUE

The servant's name was Nebibi, not that the Pharaoh Oba knew or cared. Nebibi was usually very good at senet, *the most popular board game in Egypt. Today, though, Nebibi was trying desperately to be beaten. For he was playing against the Pharaoh himself, and Pharaoh Oba hated losing.*

Unfortunately, right now Oba was losing very badly indeed.

"Throw the sticks!" Oba hissed.

Nebibi reluctantly picked up the five sticks and threw them. His heart sank. All five had landed on their unmarked sides, which meant Nebibi got to move six places – the best throw in the game.

Oba scowled. Nebibi tried to see a move

that would not capture any of his opponent's pieces, but there just wasn't one. So he captured two of Oba's pieces and gave his Pharaoh a sickly, apologetic smile.

Oba grabbed the sticks and threw a pathetic two. That sent one of his pieces to the unlucky square called the House of Water. Now it was stuck, unable to move unless Oba threw a three on his next turn.

"The House of Water," he snarled. "I hate that filthy square. I am going to pass a law to abolish it!"

At the side of the hall, the servants who were polishing the Pharaoh's gold shuddered and hurried on with their work.

Just then, the priest Bukhu marched in, his face creased into a frown and his hand clenched around his staff. Oba looked up from the game. Nebibi silently thanked the good Gods for the distraction.

"What news of my enemy Akori?" demanded Oba. "Have you found him and killed him yet?"

Bukhu shook his head. "No, Your Majesty. We searched all over the Great Pyramid, but found nothing. He was gone. Vanished on the desert winds."

Oba picked up the senet board and flung it across the room in rage. Pieces went rattling across the floor. Nebibi fled the room in terror.

"So let me get this straight," Oba hissed. "That lowly farm boy has released not one but two of the Gods our Dark Lord Set imprisoned. And now you tell me he has vanished?"

Bukhu nodded grimly. "Yes, Your Majesty, but do not worry, three of the Gods remain imprisoned, including the mighty Horus himself. They'll never defeat us – we have dark magic on our side."

"Do not worry?" Oba shrieked. "This boy has released the Gods Ra and Anubis. He has defeated the great Snake Goddess Wadjet and the mighty Hunter God Am-Heh, and now he has disappeared." Oba glared at Bukhu, his eyes glinting with rage. "How has he performed this vanishing trick, eh? Does the farm boy have a magician's powers?"

Bukhu pursed his lips. "It may be that he does, Your Majesty."

Oba turned ash-pale. "Do not joke with me, priest."

"I never joke, Your Majesty." Bukhu stared straight at Oba. "He has powers – but they are not his own. I think the Gods he has freed may have been giving him assistance. I have learned that he called up a mighty, blinding light to defeat the undead at the Temple of Horus. Does that not sound like the power of the Sun God Ra to you?"

Oba seemed on the verge of another tantrum. "But that's cheating! I see what he's doing now. He's trying to get the good Gods to gang up on me! Well, it won't work! Not when I have the Lord of Storms Set himself on my side."

Turning away, Oba began to rage against Akori as if he were actually in the room. "That stupid Sphinx's prophecy might have called you a king but you're just a low-born brat, Akori! You're beetle dung! You're nothing!" Oba shook with fury.

"My Lord, my master...my friend," said Bukhu in a voice of deep calm, "you are the one true Pharaoh. It is as certain as the stars. Look at the lengths you went to to claim your throne."

A small smile played upon Oba's lips as he remembered how he had poisoned his father, the previous Pharaoh, by slipping cobra venom into his wine.

"Yes. That boy is no match for me," he muttered.

Bukhu nodded. "Indeed. You will never be defeated, My Pharaoh. And I shall prove it."

Oba frowned. "How?"

"I have a special visitor for you," Bukhu replied, a rare smile spreading across his scarred face. "Listen – here he comes now!"

A distant boom, boom, boom grew louder and louder – the sound of huge feet tramping on a stone floor.

Oba's eyes widened. Was an elephant striding through his royal palace? And there was a smell, too… A marshy smell, hot and rank, like a reptile pit.

Then the double doors crashed open, and a huge brute of a man appeared. He was so tall he had to stoop to enter. Scaly flesh hung in folds from his body. And it was not a human head that emerged into the room. Saw-toothed jaws, yellow eyes – it was the head of a crocodile!

The servants screamed and fled to the back of the hall. One girl fainted away on the spot. The crocodile-man fixed its gaze on her still body with a hungry leer.

"Sobek!" Oba cried in delight, turning to Bukhu. "You have brought me the Crocodile God Sobek!"

Bukhu nodded. "When Set captured the Goddess Isis, he imprisoned her in Sobek's underwater lair in Nebyt. He knew that it would make a formidable prison. And now it will make a deadly trap."

Oba looked at the huge Crocodile God towering before him, his teeth as long and sharp as swords. "What do you mean – trap?"

"Well, if Akori is planning to release Isis the way he has released the Gods Ra and

Anubis, we will be ready this time. Sobek himself will be waiting for him."

"Aha," said Oba, and an evil smile began spreading across his face. Then his smile froze. "But how do you know Akori will try and release Isis next? What if he tries to save one of the other Gods?"

Bukhu shook his head. "Do not worry – the farm boy will have no choice but to go to Isis. Sobek has seen to that."

Oba frowned. "What do you mean?"

"My Pharaoh," rumbled Sobek, falling to one knee. The stone cracked under his weight where he kneeled. "Ever since Isis has been trapped in my lair, she hasn't stopped crying. I have used my powers to multiply her tears. The River Nile is starting to flood. And the sound of her wailing can be heard far and wide. When Akori hears her cries he will be forced to come and find her – and I will be waiting."

Oba rubbed his hands together in glee. Then he watched as Sobek turned to look at the fallen servant girl once again, drool trickling between his long jagged teeth.

"I have a better feast for you than her, mighty Sobek," Oba told him. "When Akori gets to your lair, I want you to kill him."

Sobek peered down at Oba, his face fixed in its constant toothy sneer. "I shall make a swift meal of him, Your Majesty, then leave his bones for the little fishes to clean!"

Oba looked at Sobek's huge jaws and smiled once again. It was so pleasurable to imagine Akori's limp body grasped between them.

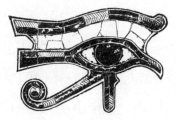

CHAPTER ONE

Under a sky the colour of hammered lead,
three young people stood waist deep in the
River Nile. They were lifting water out in
large pots. To look at them, you might think
they had been swimming, they were so
drenched. The water around them crashed
and frothed. Its spray spattered on Akori's
head and ran from his nose and chin. His
friend Manu's sodden robe clung to his
skinny body like a ship's sail stuck to a mast.
Servant girl Ebe's hair, usually a wild frizz,

was plastered to her neck and shoulders. Bedraggled and miserable, she reminded Akori of a soaked cat.

"This river is so wet!" Manu declared, gesturing at the churning water.

Akori rolled his eyes. Manu was a good and trusted friend, but he was also a trainee priest and, like many educated people, he had a knack for pointing out the obvious.

"By all the Gods, you're right! Thanks, Manu! I thought I was just sweating a lot."

Ebe chuckled, despite her foul mood. Akori liked to hear her laugh. Ebe could not speak, but when she laughed she sounded just like any other girl their age.

"Most days you sweat like a pig, Akori," Manu replied, dragging his pots of water towards the shore. "Anyone who's had to walk downwind of you knows that."

"Nothing wrong with honest sweat," Akori

called back, filling his own pot. "You'd know that if you'd ever done a day's work in your life, instead of sitting on your bony bum in the temple reading scrolls all day!"

Grinning, Manu flung some water at him, and Akori flung some back, while Ebe screeched and laughed. Then there was a sudden swell of water, causing it to lash up against their faces.

"Why do you think the river is so high?" Manu asked.

"I don't know," said Akori gravely. "Something's wrong."

Manu nodded. "Last week we had the worst drought in all of Egypt's history, thanks to Ra's sun-barge straying from its course. And now, just a few days later, the Nile is about to flood. It doesn't make sense. Where is all this water coming from?"

Akori frowned. "It must be Set's work."

There was a sudden crack of thunder. Manu and Ebe stared at Akori, then looked up at the darkening sky.

"Well he's bound to be angry now you have released two of the five good Gods he imprisoned," Manu continued.

"Yes," Akori replied. "Which means there's no time to lose. We have to find the other three Gods before it's too late."

They dragged their pots out of the river and up the shore. Ahead lay the Temple of Horus, their home and safe refuge.

Akori turned and looked back at the raging Nile. The Temple had a small jetty where the boats were moored. They had used that jetty just days before, when they had come back from fishing. Akori shivered as he remembered how a gruesome band of the undead had been waiting for them when they got there. At least since he had released the

God Anubis, the ghostly figures that had plagued Egypt had been able to make their journey to the Underworld. But they weren't the only things to have gone. The jetty had too. It was now completely submerged in water.

Ebe suddenly halted. She frowned and cupped a hand to her ear. That was one of her signs, and the others knew what she meant instantly. Akori listened, straining to hear what Ebe had heard.

The constant din of the water drowned out almost everything, but he could just about hear it, fading in and out, as if it were carried on an unsteady wind. The sound of a woman crying.

Akori had never heard grief like it. She sounded so alone, so sad. He looked up and down the river, but could see nothing except stormy waters.

"Do you hear it too?" he asked Manu. Manu nodded sorrowfully.

Akori yelled out over the river. "Hello? Can you hear me? Hello!" He waded back into the water. If the crying woman was out there, she needed his help fast.

"Akori!" Manu yelled in warning, but Akori had already waded away from the shore.

He could still hear the sound of the woman weeping. It seemed to come from all around, but there was no sign of her. Manu continued shouting at him, but Akori couldn't make out what he was saying. Up to his waist in water now, Akori strode out further – and then he saw them.

Dark shapes, swimming silently through the murky water. Bumpy backs, so easy to mistake for floating logs. A flash of yellow eyes – and mouths opening like huge traps, lined with sharp teeth!

"Crocodiles!" screamed Manu. "Akori, *get out of there!*" Ebe hopped up and down beside him, making screeching noises.

Akori didn't need telling twice. He came splashing out of the river as fast as he could. Near the shore, the riverbed was thick and muddy, sucking at his feet as he tried to run. The crocodiles swam lazily after him, as if they had all the time in the world.

Gasping, Akori threw out his arms. Manu and Ebe grabbed one each and pulled him from the river. The crocodiles clustered where he had been, so close together that you could have stepped from one to the other.

The three friends stared at the line of six silent crocodiles and backed away, in case the beasts decided to follow them onto the shore. But the crocodiles just stared back.

24

Their yellow eyes never blinked. They made Akori feel deeply uneasy.

The crying was louder now, and clearer. Akori could hear every choking sob as if the woman was standing right next to him.

"Akori, we have to go," urged Manu.

"I can't," Akori answered, anger creeping into his voice. "Just listen to her. She needs us. What if those crocodiles get her, and I'm not here to help?"

"What if they get *her*? Akori, what if they get *you*? You're the one they're staring at!" Manu took his friend by the shoulders. "How much help do you think you're going to be to anyone if a crocodile eats you for breakfast, eh?"

Akori frowned, but he knew Manu was right. "All right," he said. "Let's go back to the Temple and ask the High Priest what we should do. We have to help her somehow."

The trio gathered their pots and headed uphill towards the Temple. As they climbed, Akori looked back over his shoulder.

The crocodiles were still there, waiting patiently at the edge of the water.

And they were still watching him.

CHAPTER TWO

The blind High Priest of Horus was standing in the temple doorway. He ushered them through, patting Akori on the shoulder.

"You are soaking!" he exclaimed. "Inside with you, before you catch a chill!"

"Your Holiness," Akori spluttered as they hurried into the Great Hall, "I heard a woman crying, and there were crocodiles—"

But before Akori could say any more he felt a sharp pain in his arm. He put his pot of water down and winced. It was his birthmark, and it felt as if it was burning. He rubbed it, but that only made the pain worse. Manu was looking at him with a worried expression.

"Akori, are you all right?"

"It's my birthmark. It feels like it's on fire! I need cold water!" he gasped, clutching his arm. Light was beginning to shine from it between his fingers.

"Here," Manu said, passing him a pot of water.

But as Akori went to dip a cloth into it to hold to his burning arm, he noticed something very strange. The river water that had been murky was now glimmering, shining with supernatural light!

Could it be the reflection from his blazing birthmark? But no – the water was glowing from within. The light was a golden colour Akori knew well by now. It was the sign of

Horus, most powerful of all the good Gods!

Manu started to speak, but the High Priest hushed him. "This vision is for Akori," he whispered. "The rest of us must wait in silence." And with that, he withdrew to a bench at the side of the hall, leaving the three friends gazing into the pot.

An image began to take shape in the water. It was the face of Horus; he had the head of a hawk, and eyes that burned with frustration at his captivity. Set's dark energies swirled around him, holding him in tentacle-like bonds. Horus struggled against them, but could not break free.

Akori wished he could reach through the water and tear those bonds away, but he knew it wasn't that easy. The day might come when he would have the chance to free Horus, and on that day he would fight like never before. But that time was not now.

It was his destiny to release the other two imprisoned Gods, Isis and Sekhmet, first.

"My Lord," he said respectfully. "I am here."

"I am glad to see you, Akori," sighed Horus, his voice sounding anything but glad. In fact, it sounded hollow and anxious. It made Akori sit up and pay close attention.

"I have a task for you that is…different from the others," Horus announced. "There is more at stake here than ever before."

Akori frowned. "More at stake? How can that be?"

Horus's noble head dropped. "Your next quest is to find and release the Goddess Isis, my own mother."

"Your *mother*?" Now Akori understood why he sounded so forlorn.

Horus nodded. "Today I heard her crying. And I followed the sound in my mind to

Nebyt. It is my belief that she is being held there, underwater."

Akori felt shaken to the bone. Could the woman he heard crying down at the river earlier have been Isis herself? Despite all of Horus's power and all of his warrior strength, he was still a loving son. How horrible it must be to be unable to help his own mother. The burning feeling in Akori's arm started to spread throughout his body, filling him with a fiery determination.

"Don't worry, My Lord Horus, I will save her. What must I do?"

"Seek my mother's prison in Nebyt, and set her free," Horus replied. Then his voice became deadly serious. "Akori, you must go carefully. Trust nothing. In a prison of water, *things may not be as they seem!*"

The image of the God shimmered and began to fade. "I am placing all my hope and trust in you, Akori," said Horus, his voice becoming fainter. "As always, I wish you… good luck."

Akori nodded his thanks, but as Horus's image began to disappear from the water, a terrible thought struck him. If Isis was being held underwater, how was he supposed to reach her to save her?

"Lord Horus!" he cried. "Wait!"

Akori shook the water pot in frustration, as if that would somehow stop Horus from disappearing. But it was already too late. The shining image of the God had gone.

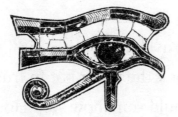

CHAPTER THREE

Akori sat staring into the pot, feeling completely bewildered. But then he remembered what the High Priest always said about moments like this: even if he was confused, he wasn't alone, and there was no shame in asking others for advice. So he turned to Manu.

"What do we do?" he asked. "There's got to be something in your scrolls about underwater prisons...right?"

Manu just looked back at him,

solemn-faced. Then he pulled out a map from his bag of scrolls and unrolled it on the table. "Do you know what this is?" he asked, pointing to a picture of some houses beside a long, snaky black line. A cluster of crocodiles had been drawn nearby. There was writing, too, but Akori wasn't able to read.

"Your finger," he joked, to stop himself from feeling stupid.

"It's the town of Nebyt," Manu continued, giving Akori a withering look. Ebe grunted as she studied the parchment.

Akori folded his arms and glared back at Manu. "Well done. You can read maps. So that's where Isis is being held – but does the map tell us how to find her prison?"

Manu's finger jabbed impatiently at the crocodile drawings on the map. "Nebyt is the single most crocodile-infested part of the Nile! There are so many of them, the Crocodile God Sobek himself rules over the place!"

"Sobek?" Akori frowned, trying to remember if he knew anything about the God.

Ebe stood up and grabbed Akori by the shoulders, pulling him upright. Then she tugged at his arm.

"All right! All right!" Akori protested. "I'm coming!"

Ebe dragged him down a side corridor away from the main hall, to where a single alcove housed a hideous statue. Manu came hurrying after them.

Akori had seen the statues of many Gods in the temple, but never this one before. It was a huge, bare-chested man with the gigantic head of a crocodile.

"This is Sobek, isn't it?" he asked Ebe.

She nodded, and looked from Akori back to the statue. Sobek's colossal jaws loomed above them, the torchlight flickering across his carved teeth. He was horrific.

And this was just his statue! Akori gulped. What would the real God be like?

"All right," he said, trying to ignore the way his heart was thumping inside his ribs, "so Sobek rules Nebyt, with all his little crocodile friends. That doesn't make him our enemy, does it? Just because he looks nasty, it doesn't mean he's against us! He might even help us release Isis, if we ask him…"

Akori's voice trailed off. Manu was shaking his head soberly.

"Let me show you something, Akori," Manu said. "See this hieroglyph?" he pointed out the symbol of a crocodile among all the other hieroglyphs on the wall. "Do you know what it means?"

39

Akori glanced quickly at the statue of Sobek. "Of course I do!"

"Well?"

"It means Sobek," Akori said confidently. *What else could it mean?* he told himself. *It's a crocodile!*

"Akori," Manu sighed, "it doesn't *just* mean Sobek. It can also mean *Pharaoh*."

"But that's stupid," Akori snapped. "How can it mean *Pharaoh* when it looks like a crocodile?"

"Just listen!" Manu insisted. "Sobek is one of the Gods who serves the Pharaoh, no matter who that Pharaoh may be! Remember Wadjet?"

Akori nodded, thinking of the fearsome Snake Goddess they had had to defeat in order to release the Sun God Ra.

"Sobek is the God who gives the Pharaoh the strength and fortitude to overcome all obstacles," Manu went on, his voice unsteady. Akori couldn't tell if Manu was angry with him, or afraid, or both. "He's going to be on Oba's side in this, along with all his crocodile servants. Why else do you think Isis is being held captive in Nebyt? Sobek is probably guarding her himself."

So, it was worse than he had imagined. Akori felt a little weak at the knees as he gazed up at the fearsome statue of the Crocodile God towering above him.

"Thanks, Manu," he said eventually, meaning it. "I'm sorry I got cross with you. I just hate feeling stupid."

Manu smiled thinly. "That's okay. I don't mind being the clever one, so long as you're still the brave one." He looked down at his feet. "I'm scared, Akori. I'm sorry to say it, but it's true. I've got brains, I suppose, but

I...I wish I had some of your bravery sometimes."

Akori blinked, and tried not to show his surprise. He had been so busy envying Manu for his intelligence that he hadn't stopped to think that Manu might actually envy *him*.

Akori smiled at his friend. "*You* wish you had some of *my* bravery? Who was it who held Wadjet back when she was going to eat me alive, eh? It was you! Manu the Magnificent!" He turned to Ebe. "And who fought off an army of mummies in the Great Pyramid, with no weapons except her hands and feet? Ebe, the Warrior Queen of the Desert!"

Akori threw his arms around their shoulders. "What are a few crocodiles compared to what we've been through together? Nothing!"

Manu and Ebe looked at each other and traded awkward smiles.

"Come on," said Akori, clapping his hands together. "We have no time to lose. We must save Isis – for Horus and for all of Egypt. I'm sure her crying has something to do with the river rising. Manu, can you go and prepare a boat for our journey, and Ebe, can you fetch us some food?"

After Manu and Ebe had bounded off, Akori took a moment to gather his thoughts. Although he hadn't admitted it to his friends, he knew that whatever horrors awaited them at Nebyt, they would be challenged like never before.

But he was not going empty-handed. The razor-sharp golden *khopesh*, the gift from Horus, still hung by his side. And there were the gifts the other Gods had given him too. Akori's hand strayed to a hidden pouch that was tied around his waist beneath his tunic. Inside the pouch were the Talisman of Ra and the Scarab of Anubis.

He thought of what Anubis had told him as he had handed him the Scarab: *It will grant you the gift of healing.*

Healing! Akori looked up at Sobek's huge jaws again, jaws that could easily bite a tree trunk in half, or crush a granite boulder to dust. It was hard to imagine any healing power in the world being able to undo the damage that those teeth could inflict.

CHAPTER FOUR

By the time Akori had told the High Priest
about their new mission, and Manu and Ebe
had returned, night was beginning to fall.
They all set off to the riverbank. A small reed
boat waited for them in the mud.

Manu noticed Akori staring at it. "I know,"
he whispered, glancing at the boat. "It's not
very big."

"Not very big? Manu, until I saw it had a
sail, I thought it was a *shoe*!"

"Okay, it's tiny. But that's the point! If we

want to get into Nebyt unseen, we need to be stealthy. Sobek's army of crocodiles will be everywhere. A small boat will be easier to hide."

"I suppose you're right," Akori said doubtfully. He looked down at the river. It was now so swollen he could barely see across to the other side. The wind was causing the water to froth and bubble like a soup and it was getting rougher by the minute. He prayed the boat would be strong enough for the journey.

The High Priest made a sign of blessing in the air. The wind rose and blew his white straggly hair across his face. "May the good Gods watch over you on your quest!" he shouted above the roar of the water. "Be careful, my brave friends. All of Egypt depends upon your safe return!"

As soon as he finished speaking there was

a loud crack of thunder and rain started to lash down on them.

Together, Akori, Manu and Ebe pulled the boat into the river, and climbed in. It was cramped, and they clambered over each other, trying to get comfortable.

"It's like trying to fit three people into a baby's basket," Akori muttered.

Eventually Ebe settled for huddling up at the prow, peering out over the waves like a figurehead, while Akori and Manu raised the sail.

Akori pushed them away from the bank. Instantly the boat went coasting off up the river, the strong wind blowing it along like a leaf. It lurched from one side to the other, making Ebe squeal and hold on for dear life.

"Nebyt's on the east bank, on the other side of the Nile," Manu explained. "So we'll head upstream, then cross the river to reach it. So long as we stay close to the shore, we should be fine."

Akori wasn't convinced, and Ebe didn't look very happy either. But they both nodded silently.

They passed villages that were almost invisible behind curtains of rain, and farmed fields where the rising waves threatened to wash everything away. There was another crash of thunder and the sky was split open by a bolt of lightning. Then a thought dawned upon Akori. If the evil god Set, Lord of Storms, was responsible for the terrible weather, then what were they doing sailing right out into it? Surely they were heading straight into a trap?

As if in answer, more thunder erupted in the sky. It sounded like one of the gods striking an anvil with a hammer. When the lightning came again it seemed to set the clouds on fire. The rain was coming down in spears now, and a puddle was steadily growing in the bottom of the boat.

"How much further to Nebyt?" Akori shouted to Manu, as they fought yet again to steady the boat.

"I'm not sure!" Manu yelled back.

"Check your scrolls!"

Manu shook his head. "I'm not getting them out in this weather! They'd be ruined!"

Akori gritted his teeth and hauled on the sail. The next second, a huge swell of water almost sent the boat tipping over.

Akori heard Ebe scream and Manu gasp. Water sloshed over his legs and into the boat. He fought desperately to steady the boat again, and managed it – but only just. There was a huge pool of water in the base of the boat now, coming up to his ankles.

And then he saw something move. In the water, between his feet. At first Akori thought it was just a shadow. But then a bolt of lightning lit up the sky and he realized the terrible truth. The water in the bottom of the boat was alive with a glowing, slithering shape – and it was growing in size.

"Wh-what is it?" asked Manu, staring, horrified, at the bottom of the boat.

"Some kind of magical snake!" Akori cried, grabbing his *khopesh*. "Set must have sent it. Keep your legs moving. If it wraps itself around you it might crush you to death."

Manu and Ebe started kicking their legs, causing the boat to rock even more wildly.

Akori stood up and began slicing at the snake with his sword. But the snake was too quick and began slithering up Manu's legs.

"Help!" Manu cried.

There was no time to lose. Akori had to

get the snake off Manu, but if he used his sword he also risked hurting his friend.

Akori dropped his *khopesh* and grabbed at the snake. Its skin was cold and slimy to the touch. Somehow Akori managed to slip his arm in between the snake and Manu's legs. Then he started to pull. The boat rocked dangerously. More water sloshed in. Ebe started throwing it back out with her cupped hands.

Another crack of thunder rumbled across the sky. To Akori, it sounded like mocking laughter. Anger coursed through his body. He would not be beaten. He had to make it to Nebyt to rescue Isis and save Egypt. He would not be defeated by a wretched water snake. With a loud roar, Akori tugged at the snake. The wriggling creature loosened its grip on Manu and sent Akori toppling backwards into the boat. Quick as a flash,

the snake slithered around him like a thick, slimy rope. Akori felt it start to tighten its grip.

"No!" he yelled and wrestled the snake onto the floor. The snake tried to wriggle out of his grasp, thrashing about in the cold water at the bottom of the boat.

"Manu, pass me my *khopesh*," Akori shouted, pinning the snake down beneath his knees.

Manu quickly passed him the sword.

Akori raised it high over his head. And then, as lightning ignited the sky an eerie shade of yellow, Akori plunged the *khopesh* down and into the snake.

There was a terrible hissing sound. Akori felt the snake give a final tremor beneath his legs. Then it fell still. Akori heaved its body over the side of the boat and it dropped into the river like a heavy stone. He sat back on his heels and wiped the rainwater from his face.

"That was close," Manu said with a sigh.

Akori nodded. "We need to get off the river as soon as possible. Let's make the crossing to the other side now, before the storm gets any worse."

All three of them looked out across the churning water. It was impossible to see the other side of the Nile now. Everything was steeped in grey.

Akori glanced at Manu and Ebe. From the grave looks on their faces he could tell they felt exactly the same as him – a deep, lingering sense that something sinister was lying in wait for them. The water snake was nothing compared to what the fearsome Crocodile God Sobek might have planned.

"Let's do it," Akori said quickly, before fear and doubt had a chance to take hold.

The wind was so blustery now that it would make sailing across the river impossible, so Akori dropped the sail. Ebe settled herself back at the prow and Akori and Manu took their places at the oars, pulling hard to draw the little boat away from the shore and out over the stormy grey waters. The further they went, the rougher the water got, and the boat nearly capsized again.

Akori wiped the water out of his eyes with the back of his hand. "Manu, learn to row, can't you?"

"YOU learn to row!" Manu shouted. "You're supposed to dip your oar when I do!"

"When *you* do? You're supposed to be following *me*!"

The sound of clapping interrupted them.

Ebe was glaring at them both from the

prow of the boat and clapping her hands in a steady beat.

Clap. Clap. Clap.

Akori and Manu looked at one another blankly before realizing what she meant. She wanted them to row in time. Every time Ebe clapped, they both pulled on the oars. Their strokes became firm and steady, and soon the boat was sculling rapidly across the middle of the river. The storm raged on around them, but Akori shut out everything else apart from the rhythm of Ebe's hands.

Clap. Clap. Clap…

Then Manu's voice was saying something.

"What?" Akori said, looking up at his friend.

"Land!" Manu repeated, smiling broadly. "We've made it!"

The east bank of the Nile stretched out in a brown bar ahead of them. The rain still pounded down, but Akori felt warm inside. They had done it! Akori wanted to leap up and shout to the stormy skies, *"You can't stop us, Set! We will not be beaten!"* But then he thought better of it, not wanting to capsize the boat in his excitement.

They pulled the boat ashore and hid it among some rushes. Manu quickly consulted his scrolls. "Nebyt is in this direction," he said, pointing up the bank.

Akori looked back down at the river. He wondered where Sobek's lair was. Would it even be visible above the water? Or would they have to get back into the boat once the storm had passed to find it? Maybe if they ventured into Nebyt they could ask someone where it was. But before he could decide what to do, a terrible wail from the river made him jump. It was the crying woman again. This time her crying was so loud it seemed as if she was walking alongside them.

"It's Isis, weeping in her prison," Manu whispered solemnly. "We must be really close to her now."

Thunder rumbled again. Akori glanced out across the river. Something was gliding along beside them, a dark mass in the water. Was it a floating log? Another water snake? In the stormy half-light, he couldn't tell.

"Come on!" he urged. "We have to find her. Let's go to the top of the riverbank – we'll be able to see more of the river from there and we can look for any signs of Sobek's lair. When we've spotted it, we can come back for the boat."

Akori started scrambling up the bank ahead of the others. But the rain had made the ground as slippery as a greased piglet. Even Ebe struggled, floundering in the mud and holding out her arm for Akori to grab.

It was a hard slog to reach the top, but somehow they managed it. Their hands and feet were caked with mud. For a moment, Akori looked down the other side, away from the river, and saw the shadowy buildings of the village of Nebyt far below. Lights gleamed from the doors and windows. Then he noticed something. The ground between the town and the top of the riverbank seemed to be moving. Akori strained to see. Was it rainwater, washing over the ground? Or the start of a mudslide?

Just then, the moon came out from behind a cloud.

Akori, Manu and Ebe recoiled in horror. It wasn't the ground that was moving. The moonlight revealed a huge, glistening mass of crocodiles, huddled so close together

they covered the earth like an ugly crust.
And they were scrabbling towards the
riverbank, straight for them!

CHAPTER FIVE

Akori had never seen so many crocodiles
in his life. And there behind them, urging
them on, was a colossal figure. Its skin
gleamed in the moonlight like pockmarked
leather armour.

At first Akori thought it was a huge
crocodile that was somehow walking on
its back legs, but then he saw the giant's
limbs and body were shaped like those of a
human, supporting its huge crocodile head
and tail. It bellowed an order, and the

crocodiles surged forward even faster than before.

He stared in horror. *It was Sobek!* They'd walked straight into a trap!

"Run!" he yelled to Manu and Ebe. "Get back down to the river or they'll have us."

Together they ran back down the bank, skidding and sliding in the mud. Manu nearly lost his footing twice, and Ebe had to steady him. But at least it was easier to get down than it had been to climb up.

"Keep running," Akori panted. "If we can get to the boat, we can set it adrift in the river. They might think we're inside and swim after it."

"Good plan," Manu gasped.

Akori scrambled down towards the water, his feet sinking into the marshy ground. The Nile was gleaming in the moonlight, and a little way upstream he saw the clump of reeds where the boat was hidden.

Akori skidded to a halt.

"Oh no!" Manu gasped.

Lying motionless in front of them, forming a living barrier between them and the boat, was a row of six more crocodiles!

Akori heard Ebe's terrified yelp as she saw the crocodiles. Manu muttered a quick prayer and glanced back up the riverbank. How much longer would it be before Sobek and his crocodile army appeared over the top of the bank? Akori struggled to see a way out of this. They were caught between six crocodiles and an entire army!

One by one, the crocodiles ahead opened their jaws, revealing rows of razor-sharp teeth. The message was clear – *you won't get past us.* They were cutting off the only escape route.

"We'll see about that," Akori whispered.

His hand went to his belt, and he loosed the fearsome *khopesh* sword Horus had given him.

He remembered Horus's words the day he gave Akori the weapon. Its enchanted blade, the God had said, was strong enough to cut through iron and stone. With such a sword, Akori would surely be able to defeat six crocodiles – but would even an enchanted blade be able to cut through a hundred more? The moment he began to tire, they would be upon him, snapping at his arms and legs. And then, of course, there was Sobek himself to deal with.

Akori swung the *khopesh* through the air, and felt a fierce pride that was stronger than his fear. The birthmark on his arm began to tingle and Akori was reminded again of Horus, trapped and helpless in his prison. The tingling spread from Akori's arm until it filled his entire body. Even if he could not defeat Sobek and his crocodiles, he could make a stand. It was time to fight – and if he was destined to die, he would at least take some of them with him!

Akori took a deep breath, and glared at the open-mouthed beasts that waited hungrily for him. He was about to yell a defiant battle cry and charge, when he heard the rattle of scroll cases from nearby. To Akori's amazement, Manu had started to rummage through his bags!

"Manu, put your scrolls away!" he urged. "We need to fight! This really isn't the time for reading!"

But Manu ignored him, pulling scrolls from their metal rollers as fast as he could.

The crocodiles were beginning to move. On clawed feet they came slithering, their bodies twisting this way and that as they advanced.

Akori took a step forward and brandished his *khopesh*. "Who's first?" he threatened. "All at once or one at a time, I'll take you on!"

The razor-edged sword shone in the moonlight, but the crocodiles weren't put off. They were still advancing! Akori swallowed hard. Soon they would be close enough to lunge at him. He braced himself for the attack.

Then, out of nowhere, Manu came charging past him, clutching a handful of scroll rollers!

"Manu?" he shouted in disbelief. "Have you gone mad? Get *back*!"

But Manu was already standing in front of a crocodile, waving his arms madly. Akori watched in horror. Now the crocodile was opening its mouth greedily, and Manu was still standing there! Did he want to be eaten alive?

But just as the crocodile went for Manu, its jaws gaping wide, he leaped nimbly to one side and shoved the scroll roller deep into its mouth, jamming it there. Instead of tearing into soft flesh, the crocodile's jaws could only clamp down on cold metal.

The crocodile thrashed furiously from side to side, hissing. Its mouth was wedged open. Its jaws tried to close with the power of a vice, but the metal rod was strong enough to stop them. The beast flung itself around, trying to throw the obstruction free, but its efforts just wedged the roller more firmly in its mouth. Manu fell back, his face beaded with sweat.

Akori let out a whoop of delight and grabbed one of the scroll rollers from Manu's hands. A second crocodile came growling towards them, and in a flash Akori drove the metal rod into its mouth. Now two crocodiles thrashed and flopped in the mud, unable to bite, and hissing in sheer fury.

Ebe hopped up and down with glee. She snatched a scroll roller and joined the others as they danced with death, coming as close as they dared to the gaping jaws and then shoving rollers in at the last moment. Manu slipped in the mud and nearly lost a hand to a crocodile's gnashing teeth, but Akori shoved in a roller just in time.

"That's all of them," Manu cried. "We've done it. We've beaten them!" All six crocodiles were in a frenzy of rage, clambering over one another and lashing their tails, but not one of them could bite.

"We haven't got time to celebrate, Manu," Akori said, picking himself up and pointing to the top of the riverbank. "There are a lot more crocodiles where those came from, remember?"

In the bright moonlight, hundreds of scaly bodies were beginning to appear at the top of the bank. Snouts wavered and jaws snapped in anticipation. It wouldn't take them long to come down the slope, and when they did...

"How many scroll rollers do you have left?" Akori asked.

Manu rummaged in his bag, and emerged holding a single roller. He gave Akori a despairing look. "We're down to the very last one!"

CHAPTER SIX

"Come on! Let's get to the boat!" Akori yelled.

"But we won't stand a chance in the water against all of them," Manu cried. "They'll catch up with us in no time."

"We have no choice," Akori said, running and slipping his way over to the rushes and pulling the little boat from its hiding place. "Isis is out there somewhere in her underwater prison. We have to find her before it's too late."

"I think it might already be too late," Manu said, pointing a trembling hand back up the riverbank. The crocodiles were descending the slope like a leathery avalanche, snapping and scrabbling, wanting to tear everything in their path to pieces.

"Quick!" Akori shouted, pushing the boat into the water.

Manu and Ebe leaped into the boat after him. Back on the shore, the six angry crocodiles still lashed and writhed, trying to get the scroll rollers out of their mouths. As Akori and Manu started to row, the sound of Isis's crying started up again. It seemed to echo, as if it were coming from the bottom of a deep well. They were getting closer, Akori knew it. He prayed they would have enough time to find her. "Follow the sound of the crying," he told Manu as they kept rowing furiously. "If we find where it is coming from, we find Isis."

Akori peered over the side of the boat into the murky gloom of the water. But it was no good. It was like staring into a starless night sky. If only they had some way of lighting their path. And then the thought struck him – they did have something.

"Keep rowing," Akori urged Manu as he pulled the talisman from its hiding place around his waist. Ra's gift had helped him before, when he had needed to release Anubis. Hopefully it would help him again now.

Mighty Ra, hear my pleas and help me, so that I might find Isis, Akori silently begged as he held the talisman aloft. Instantly a dazzling light shone out across the river like a beacon. Akori smiled. He knew the Sun God wouldn't let him down. But they would have to move quickly, as the light would show the crocodiles exactly where they were.

Ebe grabbed Akori's oar and joined Manu in rowing the boat away from the shore, while Akori shone the talisman down upon the deep, dark river.

"Can you see anything?" Manu called above the roar of the water and the woman's crying.

"No, just weeds and rushes," Akori replied, peering down into the murk.

The crying sound was so loud now it was almost deafening. They had to be close to the prison, surely. It sounded as if they were right on top of it.

Clinging onto the side of the boat with one hand and shining the talisman into the water with the other, Akori leaned right over and peered into the gloom again.

"Wait!" he cried. "Stop rowing!"

"Are you sure?" Manu asked, his voice

shrill with fear. "Look at the shore."

Akori turned and followed Manu's panic-stricken gaze. The huge army of crocodiles had reached the river's edge. One by one, they were launching themselves into the water. Their sleek bodies swam with the current, lazily coasting along in pursuit of the boat. This was their territory, and they knew they had all the time in the world to catch their prey.

"Take a look at this," Akori said. Manu and Ebe peered over the side of the boat into the light of the talisman.

There, right beneath them on the silty riverbed, half hidden by a thick cluster of reeds, was a large boulder.

"All I can see is a boulder," Manu retorted. "Please, Akori, we have to go."

Akori shook his head. "You need to look more closely."

Beside him, Ebe started waving her arms in excitement.

"What am I supposed to – oh!" Manu exclaimed.

There, carved into the top of the boulder, was the hieroglyph of a crocodile.

"Sobek," Akori announced proudly. "This must be his lair."

"But how do we get to it?" Manu asked, glancing back anxiously at the army of crocodiles, gliding soundlessly across the water towards them.

"We will have to dive down," Akori replied.

Ebe shuddered.

"It's either that or get chewed to death in Sobek's jaws," Akori told her sternly.

"Let's go," Manu said, clambering to his feet and causing the boat to tilt and rock.

"Stay close to me and follow the light," Akori said, standing up and holding the

77

talisman in front of him. "And don't forget to take a deep breath. It's a long way down!"

Akori took a huge gulp of cool damp air and dived into the chilly waters of the Nile. Ebe and Manu splashed in after him.

As Akori went under, everything went strangely silent. Only the crying seemed sharper and clearer than ever, as if being underwater made it easier to hear it. Akori looked around in the eerie glow of the talisman. He was surrounded by swirling murk, as thick as mist. Below him, the Nile's bed looked like the surface of another world.

Akori swam swiftly to the boulder. He knew there was no time to waste. They needed the Talisman of Ra in order to find the boulder, but its light would lead Sobek to them if they took too long.

The reeds around the boulder were thick and sturdy as branches. Akori's lungs began to burn as he tried to make his way through them. He thought about swimming back up to the surface to take a fresh gulp of air, but when he looked up he saw that the river above them was thick with crocodiles. They were almost upon them!

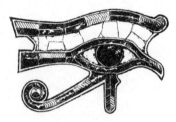

CHAPTER SEVEN

Akori forced his way through the reeds and
got near enough to the boulder to touch it.
It was even bigger up close and looked as if it
would take all three of them to move it. He
turned to look for the others. Ebe was right
by him, her hair streaming behind her in the
water, but Manu was nowhere to be seen.

Ebe noticed Akori looking for Manu, and
her own eyes widened in fear. Together they
looked desperately for him, but there was
no sign.

Meanwhile up above, on the river's surface, the crocodiles were gathering. Akori could see their long reptilian bodies silhouetted against the moonlight. They must be waiting for Sobek's order to attack! There was no way he could return to the surface now – and he knew he couldn't last longer than a few more seconds before needing to breathe!

Then, twinkling in the light from the talisman, a stream of bubbles glittered in the dark. Akori looked down to see where they were coming from. It was Manu, struggling weakly in a tangle of reeds. The green strands seemed to be fighting back, as if they were alive!

Akori reached for his *khopesh*. One good slice, and the weeds would be hacked through. But Ebe was there first, swimming down to Manu and making two quick slashing movements with her hands.

Instantly the weeds fell away, sliced off as if she had hidden razors in her fingers.

Akori and Manu both stared at her in amazement. How had she done that? How had she cut through the weeds with just her fingers? But questions would have to wait. With no more time to waste, they swam for the boulder.

Akori's lungs felt as if they were about to burst. He started pushing at the rock and gestured at the others to copy him. All three of them began to push. The boulder shifted slightly to reveal a hole in the riverbed. Akori felt a powerful force sucking him downwards. With a roar like a waterfall, the trio found themselves sucked right through the hole and plunged into darkness. Above them they heard the boulder rolling back into place.

"I can breathe!" Manu gasped.

Akori shone the talisman around. They

were in a dark, dank passageway. The muddy walls were slimy and damp, but they were no longer in the river – they were *under* the river.

"Listen," Akori said.

The crying sound was so loud now it caused Ebe to put her hands over her ears.

"Let's go," Akori said, leading the way along the passage towards the noise. Every now and then an icy drop of water would fall from the roof and land on his face, sending a chill right to his heart. Sobek must have seen where they had gone. It wouldn't be long before he and his army would be slithering along the tunnel after them. They had to get to Isis first.

In the light from the Talisman of Ra, Akori saw a widening in the tunnel ahead of them.

"Come on," he said, urging the others to increase their speed. They all started running, until they reached the end of the passageway.

What they saw there made them stop dead in their tracks. Akori put the talisman back in his pouch. He didn't need its light any more.

They had reached some kind of underground cavern. The uneven walls shone with glorious colour, scarlet and green and gold, like a box of the Pharaoh's treasure.

"If this is a prison," Akori said in awe, "it's the most beautiful one ever built."

Ebe nodded vigorously. She was looking into a gleaming dish of crystal that threw back the light in a ghostly halo around her.

"I've never read about this in any of my scrolls," Manu gasped.

Akori peered deeper into the shadows, and thought he saw something glisten. Leaving Manu and Ebe to examine the rest of the cavern, he cautiously made his way over. At the very back of the cave there was an arched entrance into another, smaller, cave.

In the centre of this cave there was a throne of solid gold. A woman sat on the throne, held prisoner by a web of glittering threads.

Akori stopped and stared, his heart pounding. He had never seen anyone so beautiful. The woman's skin was as white as the moon, and her eyes, though filled with sorrow, gleamed as bright as stars.

"Isis!" he gasped.

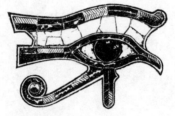

CHAPTER EIGHT

The beautiful woman lifted her eyes. A gentle smile spread across her face, and she reached out her hand, straining against the gleaming threads that bound her.

Akori strode towards her with renewed strength. The sight of Isis so beautiful and yet so helpless filled him with determination. There was still hope, and Akori had the power to make things right. He would save Isis, for her son Horus and for all of Egypt.

He reached out and took her hand in his own.

But something wasn't right. The woman's hand felt clammy and cold. Akori stared at her face. She was still smiling, but now her skin was peeling off in great strips! And lurking below was a slimy, sickly green, like something rotten in a swamp!

"Isis?" Akori gasped, unable to believe what he was seeing. Was this some kind of trick?

"*Braaaaak!*" said the thing on the throne. That was not the voice of a Mother Goddess. It was a hoarse, throaty croak.

As Akori stared in horror, the smile on the creature's face became broader and broader. It kept on spreading until it became huge, clownish and hideous, reaching from one ear to the other. At the same time her eyes began to bulge, swelling until they seemed about to pop out of her head.

Akori struggled to pull his hand away, but the clammy fingers grasped his and would not let go.

"What *are* you?" he gasped. "Let go of me!" He struggled to reach his *khopesh*, but the thing grasped his hand tightly and shook its huge head.

Then it shuddered, throwing off a few leftover shreds of ivory skin, and the transformation was complete. Instead of the beautiful Egyptian queen, there was a frog-headed woman, her swollen body as green as pond scum. Her throat swelled and shrank like a balloon. The gleaming threads that had been binding her shrivelled and turned to dust.

Akori pulled back his arm with all his strength, fighting to break the frog-woman's grip. She tried to hold on, but her transformed frog-fingers were now too slimy to hold him, and he broke free with a yell.

Akori ran back into the other cave as fast as he could. Behind him, the frog-woman bellowed in rage.

Manu and Ebe were still examining the far side of the great cavern as Akori stumbled over to them. They spun to face him. "What's going on?" Manu asked. "Oh no!"

They all looked on in horror as the frog-woman came wobbling out towards them. Akori loosed his *khopesh,* and stood ready to fight.

The creature stopped in her tracks. Her huge eyes bulged, and she seemed to be trying to decide something. But what?

"Manu!" yelled Akori. "What *is* that?"

"It's Heket the Frog Goddess!" Manu answered, scrambling backwards.

"Don't tell me," Akori cried, "she's a good friend of Sobek's."

"Worse!" wailed Manu. "She's Sobek's *wife*!"

Heket blinked, and her throat bulged as she swallowed.

Why wasn't she coming any closer?

Akori struggled to think. Back on his uncle's farm, he'd spent many lazy hours watching the frogs hopping about in the mud. They would sit and croak, doing nothing for hours, and then one of them would see a tasty fly, and without warning its tongue would flick out, and with a gulp the fly would be gone.

Heket was staring at Ebe now. Her throat was pulsing horribly. "Why does she keep staring at you, Ebe?" Akori wondered aloud, and then in a horrible flash of understanding, he knew.

Heket was getting ready to flick her tongue out and catch one of them. Of the three of them, Ebe was the smallest. *She would be the easiest for Heket to swallow whole!*

"We have to get out of here!" he urged, diving in front of Ebe with his sword ready. Heket glared at him, her buggy eyes filled with loathing. Akori glared back defiantly.

But where could they go? Then he saw a crack in the cavern wall. It was narrow – too narrow for Heket's huge frog-head, but maybe wide enough for them to squeeze through!

"This way!" Akori called, as he raced towards it. *"Hurry!"*

He waited for the others to reach him and then started edging his way through.

The gap was very tight and the craggy rock walls tore at his skin. But somehow he made it through. Akori pulled out the Talisman of Ra and its beaming light showed a smaller, wet-walled cave. The walls and floor were covered with slimy river weed.

"Quick," Akori called. "It's safe."

He helped Manu through the narrow crevice and then reached out for Ebe. But no sooner had she placed her hand in his than it was ripped away.

"Ebe!" Akori cried, but there was no sound other than a horrible slurping.

CHAPTER NINE

"We have to save Ebe!" Akori exclaimed. He
forced his way back through the gap as fast
as he could. To his horror, when he made it
back into the cave he saw Heket squatting in
the shadows, her huge tongue entwined
around Ebe's ankle. Ebe's body was draped
across a large rock, and her eyes were closed.

Thank all the Gods, she hadn't been
swallowed yet! But there was a dark purple
bruise on her head. Heket must have
pulled Ebe against the rock and stunned her.

98

Akori prayed she was still alive.

Heket's horrible eyes bulged at Akori, and she began to reel in her tongue. Ebe's hair spread out behind her as she was dragged towards the frog-woman's gaping mouth.

"NO!" Akori shouted as he grabbed hold of his *khopesh*, and the steel in his voice would have made even Set stop in his tracks.

There was a bright flash as the golden *khopesh* slashed in a rainbow arc through the air. Heket made a horrendous shrieking sound and Ebe rolled free.

At first Akori thought he'd cut the Frog Goddess's tongue clean through, but then he saw that Heket had whipped her tongue back into her mouth just in time. He wasn't going to wait for her to try again! He grabbed Ebe around her waist and called out to Manu, hoping his friend could hear him.

Heket bellowed in rage. It sounded like she

was calling out to someone, but Akori didn't understand what she was saying. The walls of the cavern shook with the force of her anger. The next moment, the fleshy blob of her tongue-tip was hurtling towards Akori!

He dodged out of the way just in time and started edging his way through the crack in the wall, pulling Ebe with him. The tip of Heket's tongue scraped against the rough rock next to them, but it was instantly withdrawn with a bellow of pain.

After a lot of pulling and scraping, Akori managed to get Ebe to the safety of the other cave. He lowered her motionless body to the floor. Her eyes were closed, and she looked as if she were asleep.

"Ebe! Oh, no!" Manu hovered his hand over the purple mark on her head, and felt her cold cheek. "Wake up...please!"

"Is there anything you can do?" Akori asked helplessly.

Manu examined her and shook his head. "Her spirit can barely hold onto her body. She needs a proper healer, Akori! I am not even a priest yet. All I can do is pray for her." He looked gravely at Akori. "And as any priest knows, prayers are not always heard."

Akori bowed his head, wishing his friend would have more faith in the good Gods. Look at how Ra had helped them with his talisman. Then Akori remembered the other gift he had been given. The Scarab of Anubis. The pin the jackal-headed God had said would give Akori the gift of healing. He took the scarab from his pouch and offered a silent prayer: *Mighty Anubis, Guide of the Dead, hear me! In the name of Horus and all the good Gods, lend me your aid!*

The scarab twitched in his hand. Akori's

eyes grew wide. As he watched, the scarab's carapace cracked open, and legs unfolded from beneath. It was coming to life!

He put it gently on Ebe's head. The scarab scuttled across to her bruise, which now looked dark and ominous. It waved its little legs in the air, and Akori was certain he heard it make a tutting noise, as if to scold a careless child who has gone and hurt itself. Then it began to glow with a soft light, like a firefly, and the tiny insect legs did something Akori couldn't see.

Slowly, the light died away. Ebe's eyelids flickered open. She frowned. Then she sat up, and the scarab – quite ordinary and lifeless now – fell from her unmarked forehead into her hand. She looked at it, shrugged, and handed it back to Akori, who was grinning and laughing along with Manu.

"I thought we'd lost you!" Akori said,

hugging her. Manu gave her an awkward hug too. Ebe looked from one to the other, beaming as if she had no idea what all the fuss was about.

Then she held up her hand, and cupped it to her ear, as if she could hear something. Manu looked confused for a moment, before opening his eyes wide. Then Akori heard it too. A quiet sobbing was coming from the far end of the cave.

"Come on," said Akori. "But this time, let's take it slowly. We don't want any more nasty surprises!"

Manu and Ebe nodded and followed. Akori held the Talisman of Ra up like a lantern, lighting the way.

In a deep recess at the back of the cave, an enormous seashell lay open. From the look of it, it might once have been the home of a colossal oyster, long since scooped out and eaten by who knows what. Now, a woman lay in the gleaming hollow. Wreaths of river weed had been knotted around her wrists and ankles, and her mouth was gagged. She was weeping quietly.

"Isis!" Manu gasped aloud, and fell to his knees.

"Careful!" Akori whispered. "Nothing's as it seems here. It could be another trick!"

Manu shook his head. "Look at her ring, Akori. That symbol on it is the Knot of Isis. It's the focus of her magical powers. Nothing else can imitate it." Manu's eyes were full of awe. "This is truly Isis. The mother of all Egypt."

"Well, you can't help her on your knees," Akori said, pulling Manu upright again. "We've come here to set her free, so let's do it!"

Together they ran to where Isis lay. She looked up at them, and the crying stopped.

Isis could not speak as her mouth was gagged with river weed, but her thoughts echoed in their heads.

My children, came the voice in their minds, as she looked at each in turn. *You have come to aid me, when grown men could not?* A smile showed in her eyes. *You do me a great honour. And you will make Egypt proud.*

But the next second, her smile vanished. A terrible crashing sound echoed through the cave. Akori, Manu and Ebe turned to see what it was.

Huge fists were tearing away at the crack in the wall, smashing it wide open. Rubble flew through the air. Crash followed crash, until with a bellow and a grunt, the mighty Sobek heaved himself through the now gaping hole and into the cave.

He threw back his crocodile head and let

out a terrible roar of triumph, his jagged teeth glinting in the light. His prey was cornered. He had them trapped now, and he knew it.

Slowly, savouring the feast to come, Sobek advanced...

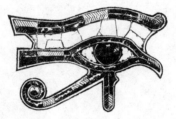

CHAPTER TEN

Akori drew his *khopesh* and stood ready
to meet Sobek's charge. With Isis helpless,
he was all that stood between the crocodile-
headed beast and his friends. *Lord Horus,*
he prayed, *I need your strength now like
never before!* His fingers tightened on the
sword's hilt.

But then two green arms appeared through
the hole in the wall, followed by the bloated
frog's head of Heket. Akori hoped the gap
would still be too narrow for her, but Sobek

had widened it when he smashed his way in, and now Heket could fit through it. She squeezed her flabby bulk up through the gap and stood behind her husband, glaring at Akori.

Now they faced two nightmares instead of one!

The two evil Gods came lumbering across the cavern floor, Sobek opening his jaws wide to scoop up anything in his path, and Heket staring with her bulging eyes, her huge belly wobbling like a sack.

"You distract Heket while I deal with Sobek," Akori cried to Manu and Ebe.

Ebe immediately sprang at Heket, hissing loudly.

The gigantic Frog Goddess took a step backwards in surprise. She obviously hadn't expected her prey to fight back! Ebe went scurrying between her huge legs and out the

other side, where she whipped around and kicked Heket as hard as she could in the back of the knee.

Akori turned to face Sobek and raised his *khopesh*. Sobek let out a roar.

"Little boy," rumbled the God, "I am *Sobek*. These jaws have bitten through the spears of the Pharaoh's enemies, the breastplates of soldiers, and the axles of war chariots! Do you think a mere flea like you can stop *me*?" He loomed over Akori, drool trickling between his huge pointy teeth. "You have insulted me, small one. And for that you must pay. With your life!" Sobek took a lumbering step towards him and the whole cave shook.

Akori tightened his grip on his sword. Next to him, Manu had begun trying to distract Heket by darting this way and that, waving his arms. Furious, Heket whipped her tongue out at him like a lash.

Manu ducked and grinned as Heket's tongue whizzed through the air above his head.

"Too slow," he taunted her.

Akori's eyes lit up – he might be a lot smaller than Sobek, but this might not be such a bad thing. Not if it meant he was faster.

"Your jaws might have bitten through spears," he taunted, "but have they ever had to deal with the sword of Horus?" And with that he started waving the *khopesh* faster and faster, until it was just a blur of gold lighting up the cave.

Sobek took a lumbering step back, blinking his big yellow eyes in confusion.

"Why, you insolent little tadpole!" he yelled.

Akori took a step towards him, swinging

the sword back and forth even faster. His arms felt as light as feathers. He would not let this lumbering, drooling God win. He had to release Isis and continue on his quest.

Sobek started chomping his jaws in frustration. "I am going to eat you, boy, and use your sword as my toothpick!" He raised one of his huge arms, and the air whistled near Akori's face as Sobek's shield-sized hand smashed past him. A clattering sound echoed around the cave. Akori gasped in horror. His hand that had been holding the khopesh was now empty! Sobek had hit the sword with such force, it was lying at the opposite side of the cave.

"*Aaaar haaar haar*," Heket cackled.

"You see," Sobek bellowed, "you cannot possibly win against me!" He took another step towards Akori. He was now so close that Akori could see a piece of rotting flesh stuck between two of his dagger-sharp teeth.

"You're nothing but an overgrown lizard," Manu shouted, racing to join Akori. "Quick," he whispered to his friend. "Go and get the *khopesh*."

"But if I leave you he'll—"

"Just go and get it," Manu said. "Without it, we don't stand a chance."

Sobek squinted down at Manu. "What is this?" he thundered. "Another morsel for my dinner plate?"

Seizing his chance, Akori darted over to the side of the cave where his *khopesh* had fallen.

"*Braaaaaak*," Heket croaked in warning. Ebe launched a flying kick at the Frog Goddess's slimy green back. While Heket turned to see what had struck her, Akori grabbed the *khopesh* from the floor of the cave. Its handle was wet and covered in river weed. As he hastily wiped it on his arm, he heard Manu cry out, "Help!"

Akori spun around. Sobek had picked Manu up by the back of his tunic and was dangling him in mid-air. Manu flailed his arms and legs wildly but Sobek's grip was too strong. Sobek opened his mouth as wide as it could go. Manu closed his eyes and started praying to all the good Gods to make his death swift and painless.

Akori held his *khopesh* aloft. Fury surged through him. There was no way he was going to let Sobek kill his brave friend. He had to stop him and he had to save Isis. He charged forwards, holding the *khopesh* like a spear.

There was a terrible tearing sound followed by an almighty roar. Sobek dropped Manu to the floor and started hopping up and down, clutching one of his huge, pillar-sized legs.

Blood oozed from the gaps between his fingers.

"You have cut me!" Sobek thundered. "Now you will pay!"

But as he hopped on one leg, Akori seized his chance and charged at that leg with all his might. Sobek wobbled and began to teeter. Akori gave him another shove and the huge Crocodile God went crashing into the cave wall, knocking his head as he fell. He gave a thunderous moan and then lay still. On the floor next to him, Manu opened his eyes and looked around the dark cave, dazed.

"Have I been eaten?" he asked.

Akori smiled. "No, you're still here." He turned and looked over at Ebe. She had taken Manu's last scroll case and was lashing away at Heket's tongue with it.

Heket made a ghastly sound of pain, and

sucked her sore tongue back into her mouth like a limp, wet rag. She swallowed hard and came waddling towards Ebe, slimy fingers outstretched.

Akori looked to Isis, hoping desperately that the Goddess could do something to help. But she was struggling, still bound tightly by strands of the same green river weed that covered the walls and floor, and Akori couldn't free her with Heket in the way.

That river weed must have strong magic in it, he thought, *to hold a Goddess prisoner.*

Then, all at once, an idea came to him. If the river weed was strong enough to bind one Goddess, maybe it could bind another!

Akori grabbed the end of a long length of the weed from where it lay on the floor of the cave. He gave it a tug; the other end was firmly rooted in the rock. As Heket came charging towards him, he dived to one side, pulling the weed taut.

Heket tripped and fell. She hit the floor with a sound like wet washing being slapped against a stone. While her clumsy limbs floundered, Akori quickly went to work. He wrapped the weed around her legs, tucking and tugging, until Heket couldn't move them. Try as she might, she couldn't stand up. She beat her fists against the floor and gargled with rage. When Manu and Ebe saw what Akori was doing they rushed to help him, and in no time at all Heket lay still, beaten.

"Quick, let's release Isis before Sobek recovers," Akori cried.

The three friends raced over to the beautiful Goddess. Akori cut through the supernaturally strong weed bindings with his *khopesh*, and Manu and Ebe pulled the pieces away. At last, Isis stood upright in the shell, shaking off the last of the weed ropes, and pulling off her gag.

But just as Isis was about to speak, Akori heard a thundering sound from behind them. With a heavy heart, he turned to see that Sobek was back on his feet. And those huge feet were stomping right towards them.

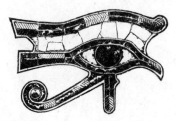

CHAPTER ELEVEN

The next moment, Akori's whole world was
swallowed up in darkness. Icy water washed
over his body, and his legs gave way beneath
him. He was spinning, falling, drowning in
a world of chaos.

He heard Manu and Ebe yelling and
screaming, and then nothing but a bubbling
noise. Had they been swept away too?

Akori felt himself being flung this way and
that by a roaring flow of water. But it wasn't
like any water he'd ever seen before. It was

shimmering brightly with all the colours of the rainbow! He started swimming upwards and, as his head broke the water's surface, he realized he was still in the cavern. He was floating on a foamy tide of water that gleamed with colours like a soap bubble. A huge wave must have struck somehow and flooded the entire cavern. Now the cave roof was close enough to touch.

Who had done this? And was Sobek still lurking under the water?

But then the rainbow waters began to drain away, gurgling and rushing into unseen cracks in the cavern walls. It sounded like the tide rushing away from the shore.

Akori ended up sprawled across a rock, wet and panting. His *khopesh* lay at his feet, but Sobek was nowhere to be seen. Manu and Ebe lay nearby, just as wet through as he was.

And there was Isis, standing with her arm raised, power shimmering all around her. A great light shone out from her eyes, blazing across the vanishing waters like a beacon. *If Isis wasn't so beautiful,* Akori thought, *that would be a frightening sight.*

The three of them picked themselves up. They all bowed in respect before Isis, who gave them a gentle smile.

"Thank you, my children," she said. Now that Akori could hear her voice out loud instead of only in his head, it seemed as sweet as honey melting slowly on his tongue.

"I have not enough words to describe your bravery," said the lovely Goddess, "but I do have this to help with the dangers ahead."

She took her ring from her finger and handed it to Akori. "This Ring of Isis will hide you from sight whenever you need it.

Use the power of invisibility wisely on your quests, young prince."

Akori smiled at her gratefully as he took the ring. "Thank you, Goddess." Then he looked around the cave anxiously. "Please, I must know. What happened to Sobek and Heket? Are they still here?"

Isis's smile became a laugh. "I assure you, they are under control! When children behave badly, they must be taught a lesson – even if they are Gods." She pointed to a large pool of rainbow-coloured water left behind on the cavern floor.

Akori peered into it and gasped. Splashing around in the pool was a tiny crocodile-headed man, no bigger than a newt. He was about as frightening as a newt too. He raged and nipped with his little jaws, and cried out in a squeaky voice. Beneath the surface, a fat tadpole was swimming round in circles, its mouth opening and closing hungrily.

"I cannot keep them in this form for much longer though," Isis warned, "so escape while you can!"

"But what about Sobek's crocodile army? Won't they be waiting to get us?" Akori felt exhausted, but maybe he could still fight, if Isis was there to help.

"No need to worry about them," Isis smiled. "All you have to do is hold hands."

Confused, Akori held hands with Manu and Ebe. He was about to ask "Now what?" when Isis raised her hand again and her eyes shone bright with magic.

"*Hekau!*" she whispered, the words of power sizzling in the air. "*Weret hekau!*"

The three of them were lifted into the air and began to rotate in a circle. They spun like a potter's wheel, faster and faster, and the cave became a blur. Manu turned pale, but Ebe squealed with excitement. Akori held on tightly to both of them as his eyes began to water with the wind and a roaring filled his ears.

"A safe journey to you!" Isis cried, and clapped her hands.

Akori, Manu and Ebe felt themselves merge with one another and with the wind. They were a human tornado, exploding through the roof of the cave and out into the endless sky.

As Akori felt himself rocketing into the starry night, he heard Isis's final words ringing in his ears:

"Stay true to your quest, young prince! Free Horus! Free my son!"

In the Temple of Horus, it had been a busy day and the weary priests had gathered for the evening meal. A cauldron of fish stew had been prepared, and was being ladled out into bowls.

The priests took their seats on benches, with the High Priest at the head of the table. He blessed the meal in silence, and everyone began to eat. One of the priests looked up as he heard a distant rushing noise but, seeing nothing, he shook his head and bent over his bowl again.

Next moment there was a tremendous crash as Akori fell through the ceiling and landed on the table. He looked around at several extremely surprised priests. One of them seemed to be wearing a soup bowl on his head. Two more crashes announced the arrival of Ebe and Manu.

Akori clambered from the table and made his way over to the High Priest. He took hold of the blind old man's frail hand. "Your Holiness, we are home. We succeeded in our quest and Isis is free."

"Akori!" declared the High Priest delightedly. "Welcome back! You must tell me all about your adventures!"

Akori and Manu began to talk excitedly at once. All the priests listened to them in admiring silence.

When they had finished, one of the priests gasped aloud. "Horus!"

Everyone turned to look.

The priest pointed to the hearth where the fire was blazing. The flames were moulding themselves into the familiar shape of the hawk-headed God. All the priests fell to their knees.

"I owe you my thanks as never before, Akori," said the flickering image of Horus. "My mother is safe. Now, you must rest. Let your friends here at the Temple care for you."

Akori nodded. "But what about my next quest? Shouldn't I be preparing for that."

"Oh yes," Horus replied. "But not before you've had a good night's rest. Your next quest will be your most dangerous yet. If you thought your encounter with water was bad, next time you will be journeying to the very heart of—"

The flames in the hearth suddenly started to fade.

Akori's heart began to pound. "To the very heart of what, Your Holiness?"

But it was no good. The image of Horus flickered and faded and then disappeared altogether in a puff of smoke.

"What's happened?" Akori cried. "Horus! Come back!"

But the hearth was now empty, apart from a pile of sooty ashes.

Akori turned to the High Priest in despair.

"He's disappeared, High Priest. He disappeared before he could tell me where to go for my next quest."

The High Priest shook his wizened head sadly. "His power is fading, Akori. Hopefully he will be able to gather the strength needed to come to you again. You will have to be ready for him if he does. He may not have long left."

"I will be ready," Akori replied solemnly. "I won't let him down."

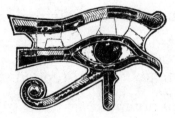

EPILOGUE

"What did you say?" screamed the Pharaoh
Oba.

"They were turned into a tadpole,"
repeated Bukhu, "and a baby crocodile—"

"I heard you the first time, idiot!" Oba
stared at his priest in disbelief. "But how?
Sobek is the mighty Crocodile God! His jaws
have crushed thousands! How did Akori do
this?"

"Magic!" scowled Bukhu. "The magic of
Isis, no doubt! She has power over life. She
would not kill – oh no, not her. She merely
made Heket and Sobek into babies for a
while to allow the farm boy time to escape."

"So, once more Akori has had help from
his wretched good Gods." Oba mounted the

steps to his throne, and sprawled sideways across it. He was silent for a while before speaking again.

"I shed blood to win this throne, Bukhu. Family blood. So why is it that nobody seems able to help me keep it? What good is my bravery if you all fail me? Is every last one of you a traitor?"

"Do not worry, Your Majesty," said Bukhu, fighting to keep his voice calm. "No amount of magic will help Akori next time. Where he is going, he will burn…for ever."

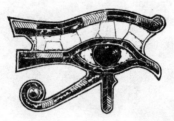

DON'T MISS AKORI'S NEXT BATTLE!

LAIR OF THE WINGED MONSTER

Vicious vultures and deadly beasts lie in wait for Akori as he searches the desert for the Hidden Fortress of Fire – and the Goddess imprisoned there. Will he survive or will this quest be his last…?

Manu pointed to the sky with a yell.
Something enormous was swooping in their
direction, blotting out the sun. Akori saw
huge wings beating and smelled something
foul and rank. He glimpsed a gaping beak, an
eye as huge as a round shield... It was a
vulture, the hugest he had ever seen. It was
circling above them, horribly silent for
something so big. When vultures circled like
that, Akori knew, they were waiting for
something down below
to die. And then they
would come and feast.

Akori reached for
his khopesh. "I'm not
dead yet," he
snarled. "You want a
fight, you'll get
one!"

ISBN 9781409521082

ALSO AVAILABLE:

ATTACK OF THE SCORPION RIDERS

For his first quest, Akori must risk his life, fighting giant scorpions and a deadly Snake Goddess. But will his terrifying battle end in victory?

ISBN 9781409521051

CURSE OF THE DEMON DOG

The dead are stalking the living and Akori must send them back to their graves. But dog-headed Am-Heh the Hunter has sworn to destroy Akori... and no one has ever escaped his fearsome jaws.

ISBN 9781409521068

SHADOW OF THE STORM LORD

The battle to end all battles has begun. Akori must fight Set, the dark Lord of Storms himself, and beat Oba, the evil Pharaoh, to claim his rightful throne. But can Egypt's young hero finally win the crown?

ISBN 9781409521099

COLLECT THE CARDS AND PLAY THE GAMES!

CAN YOUR MORTAL BEAT A GOD?
OR WILL A MONSTER DEFEAT YOU BOTH?
TO FIND OUT, JUST PLAY...

THE BIG STEAL

The aim of the game is to win the advantage by stealing the strongest card before the main battle begins!

Players: 2-4
Number of cards: at least 4 per player
Dice: 1

Instructions:
- Shuffle the pack of cards and deal a minimum of 4 cards to each player.
- *All players:* turn your topmost card face up.

THE STEAL:
- Play starts with the Magic category. The player with the lowest stat in that category, the attacker, goes first and can attempt to steal any player's card to take the best score.
- The attacking player and the defending player both roll the dice. If the attacking player gets the higher score, they swap cards with the defender and take the advantage. If not, the players keep their original cards. Play continues clockwise until everyone has had one turn trying to steal (or managed to keep the highest card).

THE ATTACK:
- The player who now has the lowest Magic stat starts, by throwing the dice for a bonus score. If they throw a number that corresponds to any of the bonus icons on their card, they add the

bonus score indicated on the icon (100, 200, 300 or 400) to their Magic category score. If the number rolled fails to match a bonus icon, they do not get any additional points.

- Play continues clockwise, with each player taking it in turns to throw for a bonus.
- The player with the highest score wins the round and puts their card to the back of their pack. All other players put their losing cards out of play.

- Players turn the next card in their pack face-up and begin a new round with the Intelligence category, then move on to Bravery and Strength for the following rounds.

- *WIN*: When only one player has any cards remaining they are the winner!

FOR MORE FANTASTIC GAMES, DON'T FORGET TO CHECK OUT THE QUEST OF THE GODS WEBSITE...

THERE'S A WHOLE WORLD OF GODS AND MONSTERS WAITING TO BE EXPLORED AT...

www.questofthegods.co.uk

Check out all the game cards online and
work out which ones YOU'LL need to
beat your friends

Discover exclusive new games to play
with your collectable cards

Investigate an interactive map of ancient Egypt

Get tips on how to write top-secret messages
in hieroglyphics

Find out the goriest facts and grossest info
on ancient Egypt

Download cool guides to the gods,
amazing Egyptian make-and-do activities,
plus loads more!

LOG ON NOW!

WWW.QUESTOFTHEGODS.CO.UK